HABITS
of
RABBITS

Written by Kira Daniel
Illustrated by Karen Pellaton

Troll Associates

Library of Congress Cataloging in Publication Data

Daniel, Kira.
 Habits of rabbits.

 Summary: A free rabbit living in the woods and a pet
rabbit living in a cage exchange places each thinking
that the other's life is better.
 [1. Rabbits—Fiction] I. Pellaton, Karen E., ill
II. Title.
PZ7.D218Hab   1986   [E]   85-14122
ISBN 0-8167-0632-8 (lib. bdg.)
ISBN 0-8167-0633-6 (pbk.)

10   9   8   7   6   5   4   3   2   1

HABITS
of
RABBITS

Daisy was a lucky white and
brown rabbit. She lived in a
woods near a splashing brook
and a field of wild flowers.

When she was hungry, she hopped to the field of wild flowers. She liked yellow flowers best. She ate them right down to the roots. When she was thirsty, she drank cool water from the brook. When she wanted to feel safe, she hid in the shadows of the tall grass. Daisy was speedy. She could run faster than a hungry fox.

"My life is perfect," said Daisy.
"I have everything I want. I
have everything I need."

One day Daisy took a short cut
to the brook. She passed a row
of houses. As she hopped by,
Daisy noticed something in a
shady yard.

"It's a cage," said Daisy. "And someone is in it."
She hopped closer. She looked inside.

"It's a rabbit!" thought Daisy.
"Rabbits shouldn't live in cages.
They should be free."

"Hi," said the white and brown
rabbit in the cage. "My name is
Victoria. Who are you?"
She looked hard at Daisy.
"I didn't know rabbits lived
outside of cages," she added.

"Oh, yes. I'm Daisy. I live in
the woods near a splashing
brook and a field of wild
flowers. I have everything I
want and everything I need."
"So do I," said Victoria.

"But you can't drink from the
brook when you're thirsty. You
can't find wild flowers when
you're hungry," said Daisy.
"I don't have to," answered
Victoria.

14

She pointed to a china dish in
the cage. It had tiny roses
painted on it. It was filled with
crunchy food.

"Two children and their father built this cage for me. They bring me crunchy food from the supermarket. They give me clean, clear water in a bottle. When it's cold, they bring me soft hay for a blanket. When I'm lonely, they pet me. They say 'hello' in the morning. And 'good night' when the sun goes down. Best of all—they love me. I have everything I want. I have everything I need," said Victoria.

Daisy thought about this.
"Looking for food every day is
hard work," she said. "No one
takes care of me when it's cold.
No one talks to me every
morning and every night."

She looked at Victoria's pretty
little dish.
"And worst of all, I don't have
even one child to love me," said
Daisy.

"Yes, that IS unlucky," said Victoria. She licked the fur on her foot.

"But don't you ever wish you were free?" asked Daisy. "You could go everywhere. You could see everything. Have you ever seen a whole field of wild flowers?" she asked. "It's beautiful—like a rainbow in a sun shower."

Victoria thought about this.
"I've never even seen a rainbow
OR a sun shower," said
Victoria. "I've never seen a lot
of things."

Victoria put her head down. She
looked glum. Daisy watched
her. Suddenly, her nose
twitched. She had an idea.

"Why don't we trade places?"
asked Daisy. "We look alike.
The children will never know.
I'll stay here. And you can go
free."
Victoria hopped up.
"Great!" she said. "Let's do it."

The next morning the children said hello to Victoria. They brought her clean water. They filled her painted dish with crunchy food from the supermarket. They petted her soft fur. Victoria felt a little sad about leaving them. But she thought about being free.

When they left, Daisy appeared.
"Hi," said Daisy. "Are you
ready? I can't wait to live here."

"Yes," answered Victoria. "I
can't wait to see the field of
wild flowers. I can't wait to see
a rainbow in a sun shower."

Daisy opened the little door to
the cage. It was tied loosely
with a smooth pink ribbon. In a
wink, Daisy was inside. She
looked at the dish with the
painted roses. She smiled.
Victoria retied the pink ribbon.

"I'll visit you," said Victoria.
"The yellow flowers taste best,"
shouted Daisy as Victoria
hopped away.

Daisy settled down to enjoy her
new life. First she stretched out
in a shady corner. She waited
for something to happen.
Nothing happened. She tried
another corner. Still nothing
happened.

"I wonder when the children will come," thought Daisy. She tapped her toes on the wire cage. She moved to another corner.

32

Victoria had reached the brook.
She crept to the water.
"It looks very muddy. And not
at all good for my health," she
said as she took a tiny sip.

Victoria hopped to the field of wild flowers. She nibbled a small yellow flower. It was a bright day. Sunlight streamed down on Victoria's fur.
"This must be a sun shower," she thought. "I wonder where the rainbow is."

She waited and waited in the
bright sun. She saw no rainbow.
Soon she felt like a toasted
rabbit.

"Maybe I'll see a rainbow in the
tall grass of the meadow," said
Victoria.
She jumped into the cool
shadows. She searched for a
rainbow. But now she didn't
even see the sun shower.

Victoria was getting very tired.
She wasn't used to all this
walking. She never enjoyed
much exercise. She stopped for a
rest.

A tall, dark shadow moved near
her. Victoria wiggled her nose.
"*Mmm*, a tasty rabbit!" said a
fox.
It pounced in the air. It caught
some white fur in its flashing
teeth.

Victoria forgot she was tired.
She forgot she didn't like
exercise. She forgot about the
rainbow in the sun shower. She
raced as fast as she could. She
hopped through the grass and
ran for her life.

Luckily for Victoria, this fox
didn't like much exercise either.
It was out of breath by the edge
of the meadow.

Victoria didn't look back. She kept racing. She raced past the field of wild flowers, past the brook, past the row of little houses, until she saw the cage with the pink ribbon.

She untied the ribbon and
opened the door. In a flash, she
was in the cage and out of
breath.

By now Daisy was tired. Tired of waiting for something to happen. Tired of tapping her toes on the cage. Tired of waiting for the children to come. Tired of being a pet in a cage.

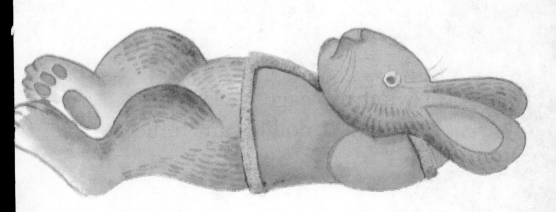

"I want my cage back," said
Victoria. "I don't want to be
free."

44

Daisy was more than glad to
hear this.
"It's all yours," she said to
Victoria. "I need to see my
fields and my brook again. I
need to be free."

45

Daisy tied the pink ribbon. She
hopped to the field of wild
flowers. It was raining lightly.
But the sun was out.

Her nose wiggled with excitement. Daisy was a lucky white and brown rabbit. Over the field was a rainbow in a sun shower.

"I have everything I want and
everything I need," she said.
And she bit into another sweet
yellow flower.